T0158118

Lullabies for Annika

Annika Tetzner

Order this book online at www.trafford.com
or email orders@trafford.com

Most Trafford titles are also available at major online book retailers.

Printed in the United States of America.

ISBN: 978-1-4669-6581-2 (sc)
ISBN: 978-1-4669-6582-9 (e)

Trafford rev. 11/21/2012

 www.trafford.com

North America & international
toll-free: 1 888 232 4444 (USA & Canada)
phone: 250 383 6864 ♦ fax: 812 355 4082

This book recognizes and honors the contributions of Bruno and Mollie Slansky to the survival of the beset and oppressed peoples of the Czech Republic during the Second World War. They and their family were among the minority of Americans who believed that any help, no matter how small, was of immense importance to all of Europe. Were it not for the powdered milk donated by them, my mother would not have survived, and I would not be here to tell the tale. This then is the story of perseverance and success.

A BED-TIME STORY FOR GROWN-UPS ABOUT HOW I LOST SCHONE ANNICA; MY INVISIBLE COMPANION IN THE KINDERBLOCK; AND HOW I CAME TO KNOW THE REALITY OF BEING A GIRL; A JEWISH GIRL . . . .

I was there when the men came, three of them on horses, cantering into the yard. I think Schone Annica thought they wanted their boots polished because I saw her smile and look at them. They jumped off the horses, and one of them took her shoulders. They were laughing, but they were angry too, I think.

I didn't know what they were up to, but Schone Annica screamed. I wanted to
Run around the corner and hide. They dragged her inside and shut the door.
And I screamed.
Nobody came.
They were drunk and said dirty words in German and Polish. Their eyes were
All puckered in their flat cheeks.
They pulled my skirt over my face.
They will smother Schone Annica, I thought
I MUSN'T LOOK . . .
Still I could not look away from what they did.
Like the dogs.
Jiri used to say don't look-and I asked why musn't I?
And Jiri answered:
Because you are too small to understand.
It will frighten you.
But the dogs had not frightened me at all. It seemed a simple thing
what they had done.
Not like this.

Schone Annica twisted and kicked, her screams under the skirt and turned
to weeping and pleading—
soft, like one of the small puppies belonging to the SS.
Two of the men pinned her arms and the third lay on top of her.
Then they changed places until all three had lain on her.
After a while I stopped moving and crying.
I thought they had killed me.
When the man left they flung the door wide.
I could hear the other children in the yard and the Kapo yelling.
The white light fell on Schone Annica with my skirt over my face.
My naked legs spread wide-bloody sticky on my thighs.
After a long while I draw the skirt down.
I was afraid to touch Schone Annica.
She was gone.
I had a cut on my chin.
Then I wished I was dead
like my mother was.
I went outside and vomited in the mud.
That is the way I remember
for all these years.
The way I would think of a man and a woman.
Although, I did not want to think of them like that.

Jiri lay down on the bed beside me later that night.
He took my hand—
his was hot and rough.
Listen to me, he said softly
Listen; I would give anything if you had not been through what you
went through today.
Such an ugly, ugly evil thing . . . .

He was trembling.
The long quivering shook his body,
shook his voice.
The world can be so scaring and people be
worse than beasts.
Still people are for the most good.
You must try to put this out of your head as soon as you can.
—Will nobody punish those men?
—In the first place nobody could prove who did it.
Nobody saw it.
—I did. And I remember their faces. Especially the short thick one. He
Wears a tie and sometimes he gets drunk together with the SS.
Jiri sat up: Listen to me-Do you hear?
You are never,
Never to tell anybody
ANYBODY—
At all.
Do you understand?
Terrible things would happen to you.
To me, to all of us.
You must never, never . . . .
I was scared:
—I understand. But then-there is nothing that can be done about people
like that?
—Nothing.
—Then how can we know it would not happen again, maybe even to you?
—I think we cannot.
—Then they can always do what they want to do.; Even kill us, even . . .
—That too. You are big enough to know.
I cried-Jiri held me. His face was crumpled and creased.

In the beginning there was a room with a table, a black iron stove and old red flowered wall paper. The child lay on a cot feeling the heat while mother moved peacefully from the table to the stove. When the mother sang, her small voice quavered over the lulling nonsense words; the song was meant to be gay, but the child felt sadness in it. "Don't sing," she commanded and the mother stopped. She was amused. Imagine, she told her husband, Annica doesn't like my voice. She made me stop singing today.

The father laughed and picked Annica up. He had a beard and dim blue Eyes behind thick glasses. He was slow and tender; when he touched the mother, the child was comforted. When he put his arms around the mother she said "kiss Ima."

They laughed again and the child understood that they were laughing At her and that they loved her.
For a long time the days were all the same. In the house the mother moved between the table and the stove. The father was sitting with his big books, or spoke quietly with other men, who lived in other rooms. On the big bed in the room back of the kitchen other mothers brought new babies to birth; and everybody had sad faces. And when, the babies were nowhere to be found, even the child looked eagerly for them.

On Friday nights there was a white cloth on the table; sometimes there was sugar in the tea, and bread. Tata brought beggars home-they were dirty and had a nasty smell. They were given the biggest piece of the bread, and two spoons of sugar in their tea. The room was shadowed; the white light of the candle burned through Ima's hands as they moved in the blessing. There was a lovely and lofty mystery in her words and on her face.

It seemed to the child that the world had always been and would always
be like this. She could not imagine any other way for people to live.
The streets through the ghetto were dusty in the summer, muddy and
icy in the winter. The houses were crowding along the streets, clustered
around the SS houses, and the grey big block which was the house of
Death. All the people living in the house here, knew you and called
you by name.

The ones who did not know you-the Others-lived on the far side where
the church steeple rose. People seldom went there. There was no reason
to go unless you were ordered or you were a SS.

The days were measured and ordered by the father's morning, afternoon
And evening prayers; by the brother in his black jacket and visored
cap going to and coming home from Shul. The weeks ran from Friday
night to Friday night. In the silence of the nights you heard the boots of the
SS hitting the stone paved street; Eins-Zwei . . . Los Mench, los. Los . . . and the
child curled close to the mother crying silently.

Annica sits on the step in the breathless night watching the stars. Of
what can they be made? Jiri says they are fire. The old grandmother
in the backroom says the earth is fire like them, and that if you could
stand far off and look at the earth it would glitter like the stars. But
how can that be?

Tata does not know; he does not care about such things. If it is not
in the Torah he is not interested in it. Ima sighs and says that she
Does not know. Surely it would be wonderful if a woman could be educated
and learn about things like that. A rabbi's wife in a far-off district
runs a school for girls. There you could learn about the stars and
how to speak other languages and much else besides. But it would be
very expensive to go to such a school and anyway what would one do
with that kind of knowledge in this place? Therezienstadt is designed
for another kind of life.

But of course, Ima says, everything need not to be USEFUL. Some things
Are beautiful for themselves alone. Her eyes look into the distance
and the dark. Maybe it will be different after awhile, who knows?

Annica does not really care. The stars glow and spark. The air is
like Ima's hair, soft. Clouds foam up from the horizon and a chill comes
skimming with the wind. Down the street comes the SS night patrol: hep—
hep-yid-yid. Tata closes the window with a clack and click. It is night
Sometimes she listens to scraps of talk, the adults evening murmur
that repeats itself often enough to form a pattern. They talk about
America. Annica has seen the map and knows that, if you were to travel
for days, after a time you would come to the end of a land called Europe
which is where they live. And then there would be water, an ocean wider
than the land over which you have come. You would sail for days across
that water in a ship. It is both exciting and very scaring.

There are many people in the ghetto whose relatives have gone to
America. Ima has a cousin in a place named New York; But has been there
since before Annica was born. Tales arrived by mail: In America everyone
is alike, and it is wonderful because there is no difference between
rich and poor. It is a place where there is equality and justice; every
man is the same as every other. America also is a place where it is
possible to become rich and wear shoes and have white bread on the
table and Ima would not watch how much sugar you took for your tea.
Tata and Ima have been talking for a long time about going, but there
has always been some reason they cannot leave. But when she asks, their
faces close and their eyes get empty.

So they would never go, Annica knew. America was only something to
talk about. They would stay here always. One day, a long time from now,
Annica would be grown, become a bride, led under the chuppa to dance the
dance of violins, with a white gauze veil over her face. Then she would be
mother, lying in bed with a little baby-but the baby would be gone. It would
be the same life; Tata and Ima would be here, looking no different from the
way they look now.

Yes, and the SS shelter would be here too. And the soldiers marching and shouting Heil Hitler. People would still be sent on transport and Jiri would be taken away. The SS like sweet boys like him.

She hears the nightman pushing his wagon through the empty streets. He is picking up the harvest of the day. Many of the small ones she used to talk to when in Shul, are gone with his wagon. But he is not to stop by her place. She knows: I am alive, I am here, and I am going to sleep.

Noch Eines Schlafenlied Fur Annika

This was my mother's song
by night
when,trembling with fear
she heard the SS men shout.
as their boots hit
the stone paved streets of Theresienstadt.
This was my mother's song
when my hands grasped for comfort
when the train headed
for the House of Death.

Shush, meine Kleine

Reuben is my firstborn
and my strength

Shush, meine Kleine

Simeon
and Levi,
Simeon and Levi
they are brothers
Ruthless weapons are their daggers—
Master of the Universe!
How I wish it was true
That they never entered our tents
for in their anger
they slay men:

Shush, meine Kleine

Your brother—
how much I wanted it
to be him,
or your father

Shush, meine Kleine

Naphtali
is a free-ranging deer
that bears beautiful fawns

Shush, meine Kleine

I will not see you grow into a delightful bride

Shush, meine Kleine

Issachar
is a sturdy ass
lounging among the ravines
he saw that settled life was good
and that the Land was pleasant—
so he offered his shoulder to bear burdens
my beloved father became a slace

Shush, meine Kleine

Asher
his food shall be rich
and he shall yield royal dainties
sorrows and tears shall be your food . . . .

Shush, meine Kleine

Zebulon
shall dwell by the sea shore
he shall be haven for ships;

Wir fahren gegen America

Shush, meine Kleine

Gad
raiders shall raid him
but he shall raid their rear.
Master of the Universe!
Make it true
that my son
might become a warrior,
most brave

Shush, meine Kleine

Dan shall judge his people
As any other of the tribes of Israel

May Dan be a serpent by the roadside
a viper beside the path
that bites the rider's hoof
so that he tumbles backward

Shush, meine Kleine

I have heard rumors—
And what kind of rumors!
Master of the Universe!
Bring Ben Joseph to your damned people . . . .

Shush, meine Kleine

Benjamin
is a ravenous wolf
devouring in the morning
dividing spoil in the evening

Shush, meine Kleine

That is what they are doing
dividing the spoil

Shush, meine Kleine

Joseph is a young bull
a young bull at the spring
a wild ass at Shur
shooting at him enmity.
the archers fiercely assailed him
but their bow was broken by the Eternal
and their hands trembled
at the mighty one of Jacob

Yeah, we tremble
at the name of the shepherd
the rock of Israel
at your father's God
who helps you—
your father cannot.

Shush, meine Kleine

Do not tremble
when you see the Angel of Death

Shush, meine Kleine

Judah
your brother shall praise you
a lion's welp
when he grows up
if he grows up
if he grows up

Shush, meine Kleine
Shush!

It was important to know who was the strongest.
The strongest was the one who decided and always was right and hit harder
than anybody I knew.
When SHE hit, I shrinked:
tighted myself around my hand like a rag.
It was like I almost wet my pants.
That would be the end of the world.
Until now I had managed.
I became like the limp kitten the boys had tortured to death because
nobody owned it.
They had crucified it on the fence—
it shrinked too.
Was only fur and claws at the end.
The crows picked out the eyes the first day.
I thought often if the cat had felt like me, that it was no place for
crying.
It only broke and broke,
but nothing came out.
Everything became too tight.

German bastard . . . .
I had heard it often.
It was something evil behind it . . . .
A judgment . . . .
The neighbors had also used that word.
Not directly to me, but when I turned my back to them: Bastard . . . .
I wanted to ask at home, but the word was a part of the danger that always
was hiding in dark corners.
It was better to forget, because I couldn't stand it.
And sometimes days even weeks could pass without anybody mentioning it.
But it came always back.
It felt like that day the other children fooled me skiing down a steep
hill, and I didn't know they had made a jump half down and iced the
rest of the hill with several buckets of water.
There was no way around when you first were in the air.
Only emptiness.
And the only thing you knew was you had to get down.

The street had its own rules.
The rules wee not always the same as the ones the adults had.
And not at all the same that you had at home.
But it was not painful more than for some short moments
as scratches on the knees or a blue nail.
So painful, your tears came at once.
But it passed. It always passed.
You didn't need to grumble, because everybody had their turn.
Olav was the biggest and strongest, but not too bad.
He had his weakness.
He was a bedwetter.
Sometimes It smelled when he had no time to clean himself before he
went to school.
I collected weaknesses—
Others . . . .
Sometimes I dreamt that I should take revenge.
really,
just there it hurt the most.
But nothing came out of it.
I couldn't . . . .

I run faster than anybody when necessary.
Or I sneaked away when nobody noticed . . . .
Jenny who worked in the drugstore gave me a lollipop because I picked
up the newspapers for her when the bus came.

Now I walked home
slowly
I looked at the sky so clear as a miracle and the seagulls played over
my head.
I could hear them scream when I wanted,
Wherever I was—
Carried the sound with me, and the color.
Sometimes the sound was brighter and more friendly than it used to be.
That made a day everything could start anew.
A day to think about good things.
A day to run fast, only for fun.
And laugh—
Or go alone with myself as company and a lollipop,
be on my way to nowhere, even I had to go home.

Jenny was kind.
I was told to stay away from her.
Jenny was a fallen woman . . .
I could never figure out what it meant.
Jenny could be rough and use a terrible mouth.
But kind . . . . always.
It might be because of her eyes
narrow with something green in them.
Alive, either she was happy or angry.
Jenny's face was like her apples.
Red . . .
the green and yellow apron never really clean.
But yes,
Jenny was kind.

If you could only belong a little, just a little . . . .
But I didn't
as I had never existed . . . .
A strange sore sensation spread around in my body.
It started with my eyes.
When in my fingers
It went so quick, reaching around inside.
Felt clammy and cold like the dead.

Maybe I had somehow started to die again?
That smell . . . .
When I was to stand up in class before the eyes of all the others: knew I
had done my homework, but still I get clammy in my hands and wet
under my arms.
The smell of half rotten flowers and death.
In the old lawn behind the school, one could hide when the weather was
cold and wet, and you didn't want to go home.
There was a little window with dirty glass under the roof.
It let daylight in, and you could see a piece of the sky.
I was thinking to take a left over candle with me, but it was no
good.
The adults always talked about the terrible thing it was to let loose
a fire . . . so she could not read or write if there was not light enough.
But nobody could prevent me from sitting under the window-listening to
the mice scratching between the wooden panel and wallpaper.

And I had stories in my head.
Many more than I was aware of;
if I was just setting there for a little while.
Some of them incredible, thrilling.
Some started the same way but with a different ending.
Sometimes I let myself suffer by giving the story a sad ending.
And I cried in the smelly old blanket somebody had left a long time ago,
cried without tears.
It was always so difficult with the stupid tears.
They were somehow locked in, and didn't want out at all.
The stories waited ready, close to the walls, in the shadows of all the
trash, between nothing.
The best had always a mother and a father coming back.
Some had a sick mother who died-in it-mothers should because they
were sick, not because they were killed.
And when the father knew about it, he would come back from a distant
foreign country and get his little girl, even he could not remember
anymore what she looked like.
Easy and simple I let the mothers die . . . . everyone said they had it
better in heaven . . . .

My thoughts were like a sweet secret.
hidden beneath a turned-over box.
Three notebooks I had snatched when the teacher was not watching-and a
pencil.
But I didn't often write down my stories.
It was too dark, or the stories happen so fast I had no time to find the
words.

And sometimes the words looked so clumsy when they were written down
that I just erased them.
It was better when the thoughts soared under the roof and around me.
They were so big.
And they were the most beautiful thing I could imagine.
It didn't matter that some of the thoughts were almost too difficult.
I had a nice story about walking along a road with a key in my
pocket.
A key for a little locked room.
Locked for human beings.
Then I always come to a certain turn in the road. There I turned and went

home to the room, despite wherever I was on my way to.
I opened the door, entered and locked the door behind me.
There were no hard hands or empty eyes.
No danger could ever find its way into such a room.

Being outside made it sometimes good that you existed.
It was another kind of life. One could run . . . Run from whatever it was . . .
If it was windy enough it felt like floating away. I just sped up a
little extra and made high jumps. When I at once became Annica who could
fly . . . .

I am a poet of the Shoa
one from the last generation
a child born to death
but out of the ashes
I raise like a fire
a torch to penetrate
the present darkness
to curse the evil
calling upon the heavens and the earth
to become witnesses
so I can myself bear this message
from the past
but also from the future
too long my voice has been silent
and homeless
but now
my words shall pound your windows
forcing you to open the doors
you will know
and will not anymore
be able to claim ignorance
or guiltlessness
you will not sleep well by night
anymore
or find peace at daybreak
but in your sleepless
dark nights
a voice from deep within
a small voice
might speak
will find yourself
lost, past
to be forgotten
behind nice, correct words
talk together
at dawn
I listen

Pink

I am gone
and I struggle
this time I am powerless
seized
I am alive
The whiteness of the room fills me
I am blind
cannot move a muscle
bound hand and foot
imprisoned on every side
cannot breathe
my head held in an iron grip
blood pushing into my mouth and nose
I am in the flesh
I am flesh
everything of the past
that comforted me
is gone, the warmth of Jiri, a body
the belief
of being home
my journey has begun
there
is no turning back.
I am trapped
by the four legged
pink monster
which fills the room
the thuder I hear
is my own heart
beating as fast as a birds
a hundred and fifty whirring beats
a minute
at least
all around me
I feel the deeper thumping rhythm
of my mother's distressed heart

the heavy pulse of her veins and arteries
around my body
and then
she slips away
I am left behind
alive
Surely it is a miracle
But a miracle is impossible
if there is no God
unless
life itself
is the miracle
but life is simply genetion
evolution
mutation
I know
I have seen it
but now
these are only long words
far away
so this is what it feels like
to be unseparable linked
to the present reality of time.

It is happening
And I am panicking
the pink monster's squeeze tightens
my mouth opens
far away
from another dimension
I hear
the voice
half mocking
can you breathe?
I know the voice?
or is it another trap?
I hear my bones crack
as my mother's blood fills me
through my body

I hear her screaming
shrieking in her agony
her screams gasp
she groans
she falters
and she relaxes
her rushing heart slows
a rough hand touches my face
the fingertips bitten smooth
the SS then
he twists my protruding head
pulls
hard
my hands are stuck
somewhere
I am going to die
he pulls again
harder
distorting my face
as I feel my lip tearing when my teeth clinched
I have no way
to show my pain

Footsteps

Jiri and I are dragged away
the filth and the foulness of our Mama
are revealed to everybody
my blood-blinded eyes cannot see
HIM
but I shall remember
to the end of my days
his enormous voice booming
is she not dead yet?
Everything to me
are my mother's eyes
glaring into the emptiness of her darkness
the frantic flutter of my heart
fills heavens and the earth
the booming voice returns
let the child live
cursed is the child
that kills the mother

Jiri drags his feet
his eyes full
of his mother's darkness
the grip of his fingers tightens
as we are pulled long the muddy path
to the house with the blind windows

The door
bangs behind us
the glooming room swallows us
as the Angel of Death laughs
his mouth pink
welcome
home
Kinderlach!

In panic
my body leaves me
as the room spins
and spins
faster
faster
faster
I could cry in relief
when
the pink, four legged monster
again tightens its squeeze
the white chamber of horror
suddenly seems homely
and safe
its silence fills me
slowly
very slowly
I can let the panic go
and
welcome the fear
my well known companion
my comrade of arms

The pink four legged monster
looks like a chair
again

Prayer

"and God created the heavens and the earth"

I want to tell you how God created earth
Of course, I know now that God did it in the beginning of time.
But that was beyond the capacity of my knowledge at that time;
first of all because I was just a child.
Second, it was close to impossible for me to understand that the
creator of the earth-which meant the camp-was God
He could possibly have created the world.
There at least was something good;
the sun coming up, warming my body and making the pain and the
stiffness of the night go away.
Sometimes it rained just enough to make the dust more endurable.
The cool breeze in the afternoon after a long hot day . . . .
Once I even heard a bird sing. My brother said it was only
imagination:
"You don't even know what a bird sounds like . . ."
That was true, but I like to think it was a bird and not the train pulling
into the camp.
And behind our block, I one day found a tiny little yellow flower
One of the big girls told me the name of it: Tussilago Farfara
But the heat of the sun killed it.
I could not make things fit together at all.
The other children, and especially my brother, told me that it was
God who had created the earth, and that I should not ask such
nasty questions.
"It's dangerous to question God", said Jiri, as he shook his fist under
my nose. It was not often he threatened me, so I stopped asking.
But I went on thinking that some how there had to be something
wrong.
How could it be that God who gave my father the Torah, and even the big
Talmud books he loved so much? I did too, they smelled so wonderful of
dust and sunshine, and had so many letters inside, small and big ones
arranged up and down and around the pages.
It was just as you could walk in, and there was no fence or SS men
stopping you—
could He create such ugly things as the earth?
Don't say it was God, please

But maybe they were right—
It could be Herr Doktor-he could certainly be God, because he was the
only one who had a shiny white coat.
And Jiri h said God had a white coat He covered the earth with.
Sometimes when Herr Doktor did his things on me, it could be so painful
that everything turned white.
And I had to clench my teeth together and keep my eyes closed so the
white could not come out; only the ugly sticky thing named blood.
So Herr Doktor was God, that was for sure.
Later on after the camp, I used to think there were two gods-one for the
Christians and one for the Jews.
And who could really know, maybe it was also one for them between.

Jiri told me how to pray:

I knew the Sh'mah: Sh'mah Israel, Adonai Elyoheinu, Adonai
Echad . . . Amern, Hear oh Israel, our God is One.
I really knew that one . . . and many others also.
It was most beautiful when Jiri prayed.
He would rock slowly back and forth;
he closed his eyes and looked like he was somewhere else, far, far
away, and I became afraid he would leave me; he looked like he was
about to drift away and leave me behind.
I used to grab his hand, so God woudl not take him.
"Jiri come back" I yelled "come back . . . I don't want God to have you . . ."
but God took him at the end anyway-when the SS men hanged him . . .
After the war, when I ended up in a strange country, I really did not know
what to believe. I lived in a Christian home. There they prayed to somebody
named Jesus and every Sunday they went to church, I had to go with
them.

The beautiful Sabbath evenings and my mother lighting the candles
became only a faded memory.
All that I heard now was that the Jews-and that meant me too, were a
doomed people and we all had to go to a place named hell.
I thought it was not too bad, it sounded very much like it was in the
camp. Of course, by now I knew that the earth was the whole world and not
only the Kinderblock and gas chambers and starving, but I was of course
very little when I believed such things.

All the Christians went to heaven-if one was good enough . . . I didn't care so much for that heaven anyway . . . all the harp playing there was not for me. And I didn't like the thought of sitting on a wet cloud and all the singing. And forever? No thanks!

If heaven on the other hand was a big library-that could be quite a different thing! I always loved books-like my father-I still do.

Books are not like people, books don't lie. If they lie, it is because the people who wrote them lie.

The letters stay neatly on the white paper and there is order in them. And you can mix them. My father who was a very learned man, said if you didn't understand them, you could always turn the letters around, and in that way find their true meaning.

I loved to do exactly that.

The people I lived with didn't like me to read too much nor did they like all my questions, though-I never meant to be nasty.

When I didn't hear the Jewish prayers anymore, I gradually forgot the words and the Hebrew.

Not the Sh'mah-but most of the others.

It mad me so afraid. It was as if I lost the grip on what was mine; my mother and my father-and worst of all, my brother Jiri.

Of course I knew all of them were dead, but somehow . . . when I prayed . . . it kept them alive. They were not dead . . . really . . .

Maybe it was they who were alive, and I was the one who was dead.

And all the time I read . . . books of all kinds

I tried to fill the emptiness inside with them.

But the loneliness never disappeared . . .

it became even worse every time I closed the book . . . .

There were
besides parts of cadavers recklessly deposited from one end of the room to the other
a severed foot
a hand empty of blood
a chunk of brain
its gray coil moistly glimmering
glass bottles shelved in methodious order—
one with eyes, staring.
More intolerable than the sight of all this grim destruction
was the smell
it was the smell of formaldehyde
and feces
squeezed off of the crushed bodies,
and of the lingering odor dead flesh exposed to room temperature.
The overpowering stench to which nobody could easily adjust
hit me so my body almost doubled
heaving again and again.
But the sour taste in my mouth brought me to my senses
I run
Death
Death
the word pounded in my head
THIS is death
Death
the brutal reality of the place I called home.
Hiding behind Jiri's back
I shivered under the blanket
Hearing the sound of the other children in their sleep.
I knew there was nowhere to run.

copyright 2001 annika tetzner

My shadow sings in the morning
Together with the birds
From a long long time ago
My feet move easily in the new grass of spring
The air crisp and new
Making me drunk and excited
—larks are playing
Soaring higher and higher
To sing
As the pale face of the sun
Is just to be seen
The song swans lift their necks for their love song
Slowly moving their wings in a silent dance
They greet the cold breath from the land of purity
Faithfully they make their journey
To the uttermost desolation
Again and again
Making love in the House of Death
Nesting their eggs
Full of promises for a new life
Lifting my face towards the rising sun
Its gentle warmth touches my lips
The sky endless clear

My shadow is quiet
As a newly weaned child
By its mother's breast
YET
An aching pain
As the swans slowly disappear towards the horizon.

Polemides

Polemides
the frightful, beautiful child
born of the tide of war
strong and brave
beating your shield
forcefully
with your spear
Polemides, you frightful
beautiful child
of war
the firebrand gave
the grass crown
and the strong bow
to my frightful
beautiful child
of war
in the silver light
the iron strength is found
then nightfall comes
with the evening tide
and with the twilight
Polemides, my beautiful child
of war
is just a frightened
little child
helpless
and so terrible alone

I cannot remember exactly the day
I knew what it meant to be born a Jew.
In the same way
I cannot remember exactly the day
I knew the small things on paper
were a language to be understood—
that the letters neatly lined up on the white, clean paper
in the same way as the Jews were kept in the ghetto—
were kept between the ghetto of two covers.
Reading for me
became so natural, as breathing and sleeping,
still I do remember the time
when the art of reading was still a mystery.
But deep inside
I recognized the power
that forced me to teach myself to read . . .
Armed with the knowledge,
books became as important
as life itself.
A burden often;
the never satisfied longing
for learning more,
always more.
The choice of refusing to accept final, ready-made answers
to all my questions,
stumbling along
the unknown road,
there doubtful thoughts
are the milestones.
Never seeking the goal,
because the road
itself
was the goal.

This is how
I too,
became
The always wandering Jew.

Death has two mothers
dancing together
in a slow
tango jalousie
even when they turn
their backs on each other
the steps
are chorographied
in a perfect
disharmony

death has two daughters
one a flame
one ice
they look
at
the mothers
their feet aching
to dance
but dare not

death has two sons
one was love by his mother
as he went off
to the battlefield
returning
pale and stiff
in a coffin

the one who stayed home
carried his brother
till the end of his life
yet his mother hates him
he survived.

I am the clay
I am the fire and the salt
the water and a piece of bread.
I am the white and the red
and the green and the blue
and deep within, the purple of the days of old
a pillar of salt
meant to be
doomed and condemned
hell far too good.
Out of this darkness
raised a jammer
terrible loud
echoing to the boundaries
of the universe.
Still it seems that there is not space enough
for this jammer
present and past
carried for so long
this jammer belonging to me
and my lost comrades
yet
if room was to be found beyond hearing
of ONE knowing witness
when we bridge
to the other side
to the living
breaking the gates of Hell
my dead comrades and me.
I shall dance slowly and grave
for all my dead friends.

Ismael, my lost brother

Ismael, my brother
Where are you?
I cannot find you,
it is so dark here
Ismael, my brother,
is it true
that you want to kill me?
The other children say so,
but
I cannot
understand
Why?
Ismael my brother;
We have played together,
Together—
cheated Dr. Mengele
together—
Ismael, my brother, what is wrong with us?
What is wrong with
Me?
why cannot you be my brother anymore?
I was proud of you
in your new uniform;
but all that you answered
when I told you so was
"Sieg Heil, Sieg Heil"—
and
'Heil Hitler!'

Ismael, my brother
I have lost you
and I cannot even say the Kaddish—
Oh Ismael, my brother—
If I only could have died in your place—
Oh Ismael, Ismael . . . .
my lost brother . . . .

Angry

I am angry,
that is all that I know.
Spinning behind my eyes are the colors I fear most.
Drumming against my ears is the terrible sound of my mother's scream.
I hold my fists hard, hard at the ears,
trying to get the terrible sound to go away.
Her screams fill the world, threaten to wipe me out.

I am angry
that is all that I know
I want to stop her screaming,
stop her frightening me,
to hit her in her mouth to make her silent.
Hit hard so she bleeds.
Why can't she be quiet?
She always tells ME to be quiet.
Silence is the most important thing in the world.
If you love me, she says,
you bring me silence.
And I try, even I don't quite understand what she means and wants
And now—
she screams
And screams.

I am angry-angry-ANGRY
and horrified.
Because of the smell and the noise and all the people
My stomach tightens,
I want to throw up, just right here.

I looked at Jiri for help, my big, big brother.
And I knew I couldn't open my mouth.
The sour taste of vomit made me swallow and swallow.
Suddenly that became the most urgent thing;
to swallow.
Because Jiri screamed.
There was a big black hole in his face where the cracking noise came out.

My hands went to my face to make sure there was no hole so the scream could slip out.
My fingers found their way to my eyes.
My thumbs punched into them to get them out, so their holes could close.
But the sudden pain didn't make the pictures go away.
They became even more intense and hard colored.
I open my eyes again.
They took in the grisly scene I was part of:
my mother lying on the grey cement, with her head in Jiri's lap.
The red flow pulsing out of her belly.
I wanted to throw up again.
Swallowed as for my life—
swallowed hard, again, and again, and again.

Then I became aware of the blood dripping slowly from my hand.
and I wanted to hurt my mother.
me, not the big SS-man.
It was not his business,
it was me she had hurt.
My anger took my breath away,
and it turned into a whitening pain as I watched the light disappear from her eyes.
And suddenly all that I wanted was to curl up to her breasts,
and she would open her eyes and look at me,
and laugh
and tell me it was all just pretending.
And she would kiss me all over my face and tell me she loved me,
I whimpered
she had gone away from me,
to some strange place I didn't know how to find.
And she would not come back to me.

I whimpered again.
A hard blow to my ear silenced me.
Jiri said nothing . . . .
nothing . . . .

If There Be Thorns

If there be thorns
and blood
and sorrow.
If there be tears never cried
grief
and fears.
If there be hiss of death
and guns
and
a gallow.
If there be smoke and fire
aloneness and ashes.
Then
Let it be thorns
and bloody sorrow.
Let it be tears, never grief.
Let it be hiss of death
and guns
and
a gallow . . . .
If there be love
togetherness
and
a name.
Then
out of the ashes
out of grief and fears
and bloody sorrow.
The tears never cried
shall shine
on the road home.
There will be music in the House of Silence
the thousand candles never lighted for Shabbat
will sing . . . .
and I shall dance.

There is a little girl in
Me who refuses to die
despite
the sticky smell of burned flesh
and
children screaming at the Umschlagplatz
silenced into sobs
adults who panic and steal their bread
kapos with hard hands
and
empty eyes
she does not know if
there is something else
outside the barbed wire

even the world is still dark and dangerous
she refuses to die.

Mothers

I don't like mothers
honestly and really
mothers are dead
or they are gong to die.
I would have liked my mother much better
if she was not a mother.
Mothers are stupid
they don't know anything,
not even how to hide.
I could
have hidden here
somewhere
and given her my bread.
But that is the way it is,
Mothers are stupid
and they die.
They don't know to be clever
so they are gassed
and go to the ovens
and get burned
and then
they are all dead.
My mother was not gassed
and taken to the ovens.
She just lay there
and bled all over the grey cement.
Even Jiri says she is dead.
I am sure she is not dead.
She just left
went to somewhere I don't know.
She did not say goodbye
so it cannot be far away . . .
I want her to come back
and see I am big girl now.
The wolf in my stomach growls,
But if you put a pebble in your mouth, a small one,
and keep your mouth busy
the wolf gets silent again.
It also helps you.

I wanted to go and see if mama was on the transport.
He was angry, I can tell.
Gott In Himmel and Donnerwetter
and Blumensuppe.
How he gets angry!
He boxed my ears
and he screamed.
It is not his business to beat me
that is the Kapo's job—
Mama is dead,
get that into your head!!!
and he scrambled away.
I couldn't find him for a long time,
but I am going anyway
to have a look . . .
There are many big people in the wagons
many small ones too.
I hope they don't send them over to us.
but I think I don't have to be afraid of that—
the new ones don't often come to us.
Herr Doktor knows there are not beds enough for all these new people,
but the gas chambers have enough places.
Every day there are long lines outside them.
The big doors swallow them all
all the time.
I do look carefully at the big people,
But even when I close my eyes a little to see better
I cannot see my mother.
Maybe she will be on the next train
maybe . . .
I see many grown-ups
they are mothers I believe,
they have long hair and breasts
and smaller and bigger children cling to them.
I can hear them cry and whimper.
I secretly laugh
when I hear the mothers say
everything will be okay
we are just to have a shower.
Hah! How stupid can you be?

You are going to die
that's it.
Sometimes we talk about stupid grown-ups
and Chaim says
their brains flow out together with their tears—
tears are the water inside your eyes—
that is why big people are stupid,
especially mothers,
but even if she is stupid
I want my mother to come back to us.
I want, want, want her . . .

I have to swallow hard
hard many times
to fill the empty hole inside me
the hole where my mother should have been

Death

The ones who killed me
are there—
somewhere lurking in the dark,
waiting—
I am lying on my back
naked and still.
Stars on the night sky
bodies are falling
out of the darkness.
I race like the star light
and keep silent.
I am gone—
the one who gassed me
knew what he was doing
—but now
I am gone.
My body lies on the muddy ground
like my discarded garment.
Somebody bends close and listen
I can hear the shadow
it breathes within
deep in the dark
Is it the Angel of Death?
I must not listen . . .
I keep my eyes closed
It is cold—
lifting my hands—
my fingers touch my face.
I am dead.
This is to be dead.

I hear somebody is shouting
the voice is familiar—
somebody I might have known
a thousand years ago
yesterday—
I try to hear what it says.
I open my eyes
only a little.
I see the red and yellow
glow,
The smell hurts my throat.

Schlafenlied Am Annica

Now she lies here,
on her back, naked.
Still her blank stare fixed on the night sky.
The black of her pupils blown wide,
and in them
the stairway we descend;
bodies falling out of the darkness—
shards of star light;
silent as light,
quietly as pain.
But she is gone,
the ones who killed her knew what they were doing,
and now she is gone.
She left behind the form
she labored so hard to protect,
it lies on the floor like a discarded garment.

And the sea grows old in its bed.

When I bend close and listen,
I can hear the shadow of her life,
fading, yet singing,
it breathes from within a deep inner dark,
the shadow of death.
And quickly I step back.
I must not listen too closely.
I must not listen, or I will lose my soul
before I find hers.
Where to look?
Where else but in the world she occupied?
She is here,
somewhere.
The music in death's shadow
has awe and enormity within,
that gleams with cold emotion,
and with violence.

And the sea grows old in its bed.

A wolf crying at its own echo.
The soul is lost in these sounds.
And I go alone to find her.
even through the darkness
I can see the footprint of her killers,
their track leads me through
the comfortless dark.
They leave no more tracks,
they wade through decades of shadows.

And the sea grows old in its bed.

The camp's dock lamps reflect
like an angel's fiery arm
that extends across a stretch of silence,
and hands me a cry.
The ghosts come back to me
with whimpers of exhausted pain
and shadows flickering of life.
I can feel my way toward her,
and smell the fragrance of rage,
the killers have completed their work,
night spills around them
with its dirty smell.
The evil red eyes of cigarettes puke in the dark,
where the killers smoke
to cut the sour miasma of death.

And the sea grows old in its bed.

I have come for her soul,
and find her
on the muddy bottom of a pit,
shivering,
full of perplexity and pain
beyond forgetting.
The killers have ruined her,
yet still she lives.
Within the glass sphere of her inner being
new shapes swirl,
as another form of life were possible.
But no-no-no.
She is deformed.
Never again will she fit
into a form of a human.
Never again will she dance for us
under the spring moon
or roll in the dust of summer,
or chant happy songs
before the long blocking twilight.
A part of her soul is dead.
When I touch it,
it feels like deep isolation,
and cold.

And the sea grows old in its bed.

Sadly, I lower her back
on the muddy ground—
and she cries.
O how she cries.
A great sense of distance
opens in me.
The force of her life swells with her cries,
then vanishes like wishes.

And the sea grows old in its bed.

The shadow of her secrecy remains;
the shadow of death.
The very shadow captivates me at her body,
and holds me fast.
The vacancies of her soul hold me here,
filled with a dark music
that speaks of her,
and I will stay here for a long time,
haunting this ground,
linger where her body died,
where one cannot remove ones gaze
from her face
with its splattered blood
welded in rays.
For a long time
I will remain here,
listening to the floating echoes of her despair.

And the sea grows old in its bed.

I will wait for her killers to return,
return to the scenes of their crimes,
and while I wait,
the music will speak to me
as though the soul
were just a song someone played.
She was a wild child
when we found her,
we saved her from the beasts,
it gave her power over the dark forest.
And she danced for us,

As the sea grows old in its bed.

Nothing binds me anymore,
now when she is gone.
Nothing, but the shackles of time,
as I am working hard
to break those.
It was my fault she died.
I was chosen among others
to help her,
because they said I was strong,
and she trusted me—
o yes, she trusted me.
I failed,
failed because I miscalculated evil,
and did not see
how she scared others.

And the sea grows old in its bed.

Desire, dreams, and death
That is what they saw in her,
and yes, she scared them.
The wind talks to the sky,
the trees talk to the wind,
and she talked to the trees,
and tell their secrets,
talking to the unseen,
singing peoples pain
and hearing their wounds.

And the sea grows old in its bed.

I have cut through the shackles of time,
left that weary world behind,
and climb a ladder of stars,
into your world,
feeling no nostalgia for the cold reality
I leave behind.
My grief growls to a blood red moon,
And I-I rise above
Toward fathoms of light,
soar into a new world—
beyond death's fences.

And the sea grows cold in its bed.

I Have Always Thought

I am dust and ashes
and long time dead,
but under the dust and stinky mud
flame colors
white and red
blue and green
and a deep, deep purple
like a painting
long time lost
hidden behind
an eternity of dirt and fat fingerprints
with cracks
spots of something
with likeness of blood
sometimes—
once or twice during the centuries
somebody passes by
glances and turns away;
even giving an angry kick
to the worthless scrap—
grumbling under their breath:
the damn municipality should straighten up the lazy street cleaners.
—But if only one
who just passed,
would stop, tarry
and come back for having a second look:
"It might be something of value,
that sometimes happens—"
And I might be taken in
from the cold and that darkness
of endless aloneness.

It should be somebody with eyes
seeing me
—not my funeral—
an Antigone who would not bury the dead this time;
but let me seek for my keys to the gates of Hell
for once again crossing the fields of the dead
to find the pathway
to the world of the living.
The disease that had
ultimately
usurped my soul
was going
to be
terminated.
That the cost was enormous
didn't count.
In a matter of moments
I would be free
and
alive.

I lighted a candle for Shabbat
from the tiny flame flickered light
across a landscape
giving it light.
It almost felt like
Somebody was waiting
for me
somewhere else.

I rose from my chair
walked
and walked
trying to make the room
I was in
to the whole world.
My heart pounded
And fluttered like a butterfly
caught in a fist.

I walked and walked
the room I was in
became a quiet world
not yet cracked open
not yet born
no bad things have existed there
yet
and no good things.
No sun, but the fertile earth
circled by the deep blue of my brother's eyes.

Jiri
I whimpered
Help me to be alone . . .
In his extreme exile
he heard my voice
touched with life
like a gentle hand on my arm.
I felt his presence
turning, startled:
Sure—
I would see him.

But there was only the golden flame
of the candle
and the shadows on the wall.
Then in sorrow it came to me
that all the blue was
the blue of his eyes
and all the gold
the beauty
that belonged to my brother
the only one,
beloved by me.

Death is a change of colors:
the burning redness of his bleeding body
for the wan clay
of an earth bank.
His whitening bones in the abandoned camp
for the powdering white of snow stars
and the blueness of his eyes
for the clearness of an indigo sky

The circle of life is not broken.
I will have my brother
The only one
beloved of me—
forever.

In accepting change
I shall regain
what is mine:
The victory
of life.

God created heaven and earth
and the earth became dark.
Man came from man—
God became dust,
and was gone.
One morning,
I was so hungry that my stomach screamed
like the SS and the Kapos—
Just there
He was
I mean
it was
behind the Kinderblock,
I found a little flower
raising its head proudly
Tussilag Farfara, the others said
the sun burned it
and it was gone.

He was the master of the earth
the great Dr. Mengele of Auschwitz
maybe God was left behind,
in Therezienstadt—
among my father's big folios?
Hidden among the letters on the yellow pages
smelling so beautiful of dust.
The words not to be uttered
the unspoken not to be said.
I bring from the House of Death
Words never known
to shake the heavens and the earth
make the gates of Hell testify
reveal the secrets
which made the House of Death
into the House of Silence.
I speak for my dead comrades.
I survived
I speak
and
I accuse

voicing my friends
my dead comrades,
they will not any longer
stay silent.
I speak
you listen.
I will make the dreams and horrors alive
for you when you look
you then will know
you cannot anymore plead ignorant.
The earth is man's home
from its dust he was made
to dust he will go
all what he has done
will fade
and turn away.

The earth is the home of man's child
through the centuries
from its four corners
you can hear a child laughing
screaming
the earth was meant to be mankind's home
but he turned his back on it
building nests among the stars.

The earth should be the children's home
they cannot find it
calling for the heavens and the earth
to witness
what man did to the earth.

Give me this mountain
this mountain I have climbed
until my hands and feet bled.

Give me this road
this road I have travelled
until my heart became sick.

Give me this ocean
this ocean I sailed
until I lost sight of daylight.

Give me this tune
this tune I played
until my heavy thoughts danced.

Give me this voice
this voice who was homeless.

Give me this memory
this memory which is my birthright.

I will climb this mountain
with you.
I will travel this road
with you.
I will sail this ocean
with you.
I will sail this ocean of sorrows
with you.
I will play my tune
for you.
I will let my voice be heard
by you.

My bleeding feet and hands
my sick heart
and my heavy thoughts
the tune I play
and the dance I learned
in the House of Death
I will let you see it all—
Even you might betray me
I will let you see them all.

But Antigone
might still remember
the dead
maybe she still buries the dead.

I hear them,
a hundred violins
playing their soft sordin
whispering through the dark
floating around me
a warm blanket
covering the wounded thoughts
lifting up
let me fly
over the hills to a distant land
the land of the living.

Small, thin hands
touching the strings
they cry
they wimp
telling strange tales
from the House of Death.
Their songs leering at me
over the brim of the cup
drinking it empty
without breathing
their dark look:
Remember?

I hear the hundred violins
their melancholic voices
painting waves of colors
the white and the red
the green and the blue.
I see the tune
and hear the colors
of the hundred violins
sometimes
a distant echo
then
a anatol symphonic thunder
then
a still small voice
a small voice,
yeah, but not lost.

The hands are still
waiting
The violins silent
speak for us
speak the unspoken

As my heart cries
I play my Viola da Gamba

There are footsteps in the garden
the sound cannot be silenced
it is my comrades seeking me
pounding on my closed gate
let us in
let us in
bring us into your time
let us in
Let your words
become flesh on our burned bones
your brushes
recreate the light of our broken skin
and
life to our eyes lost in darkness
There are footsteps in the garden
the light treads
of small children
eager for breakfast
and play
their laughter drifts through the crisp air
of a newborn morning.

These big boys with hands deep in their pockets
slowly shuffle nearer
too shy to openly show
their eagerness for life

These footsteps in my garden—
the sound of them
like
smattering guns
or
marching boots
my early morning guests
scatter
like frightened crows
dark wings cloud the brightness of the sun
their hearts pounding
fast, fast, fast
breathless whisper:

Death came too!
hidden between flowers
and dead leaves from the autumn
Their echo drifts
towards your eyes
in the twilight
of tomorrow
and
a yesterday
when you open the book
my dead comrades
left behind

Remember
There are footsteps in the garden

For the price of a child

for the price of a child
you can enjoy yourself
oh yeah!

for the price of a child
you can get what you want
oh yeah!

for the price of a child
you can always get away
oh yeah!

but then the tent is empty
and everyone is gone
oh yeah!

even the clowns who were painted
in dirt and tears and blood
oh yeah!

the price you paid
for the child
oh yeah!

has left you alone
oh yeah!
you child of None
oh yeah!
oh yeah!

A House For My Dreams

I shall build a house for my dreams
with windows and doors
so my dreams can walk out
and walk in.
In the garden, flowers will sing
and the birds dance.

In the backyard you can catch
the stars in the creek,
and weave yourself a dress
from a spider's silver web.
The moon laughs at the sun,
and the honored guest of the evening
is the gentle breeze.

When the party is over,
and everyone gone.
I will stand in the doorway
and say goodnight
to the silence of the night
before I go inside
and close the door.

Anus Mundi
Or Give Me Today My Daily Bread

September 9, 1942

Today I see colors again.
—The terrible, dark cloud
is drawn back from my life:
I get my divorce:
Can you believe it?
It has to be celebrated.
And I think the menu will be:
tomato soup,
half a hen with potatoes,
red cabbage,
sweets,
and the excellent vanilla ice cream—
but these children
outside the block,
their screams
about
how hungry they are,
that kills my appetite—

8 pm: a Sonderaction.
you know,
the one practiced here,
burning the inmates alive—
especially useful
when it comes to the children—
now everybody is on duty.

Five cigarettes
Hundred gram sausage and bread,
certainly good for these brave men
Oh-these children;
Their screams and demands for food
kill my appetite.

September 10

This beautiful morning
—has to supervise a gas chamber action,
but today mostly older inmates
a great contingent of children.
It is well and good,
the children's crying disturbed
my otherwise excellent supper.

September 12

Sonderaction:
1700 children,
—got soap flakes and TWO pieces of soap,
A wonderful concert this afternoon,
bright sunshine—
It was really a once-in-the-lifetime experience.
The prisoner's band was to be exterminated
afterwards.
Eighty musicians,
their conductor a once famous one
from Warsaw.
—For supper we had pork.
But these children,
suffer, small children?
Do not worry—
it is different for them
when they are small
that they do not have a language
to explain.
Do not worry
you can make a child to believe
whatever you say.
These stupid, small monsters
actually love you.
You can put a milestone
around their necks—
these thin, pathetic necks—
bowed in obedience

so easy to snap.
—children are not reliable witnesses
—you know that.
they always think THEY are the guilty ones.
Suffer small children?
They actually ask for it
these small, cheap monsters
they are hopeless—
they should be silenced,
their screams about food
kills my appetite.
I have a sensitive stomach, as you know—
All my love to you,
and our small ones.
and
a nice box with real coffee
and sweets for the children.
You see
we had a good razzia today.
Auf wiedersehen.

The snow had melted
and turned the frozen ground into mud
The grown-ups talked about spring, whatever that could mean
there was no life to awake
only destruction and death
outside the camp the black frames of burned-out houses
pointed their crooked fingers to the grey clouds
there were no mother birds
to nest
or kittens, only the nasty rats, everything else was slaughtered
there were no seedlings planted
the men to tend the fields were dead
no mothers planned their spring cleaning
they were too busy with gathering their things together
the curtains to take down for washing had long time ago been cut into clothes.

THAT woman towered over me
looking strained and angry
her voice sounded somehow dangerous
as she told me to get up
when her hard hands stripped off my clothes
my stomach was heavy:
was I to be taken away again?
The red navy dress and the thick stockings which always itched so terrible
were ready on the bed,
scared me even more
I just knew something terrible was about to happen
but I knew better than question it.
My ribcage became too small
to keep breathing
my stomach tightened into the well-known knot
of fear
SHE held my hand so hard
It hurt
I try to hang limp
a blow to my ear made me change my mind
obeying, I tried to keep up with her.
The big train pushing and blowing out steam, the noise of the crowd
made finally my question to burst out:

am I on transport again?
Something soft flickered over her face
then gone
A hard push behind
sent me up the high steps
and sent me stumbling into the wagon
half blinded with non-tears
I was pushed into a corner seat
A whistle blew sharply outside
soon the people on the platform fade in the mist

The train swayed slowly
side to side
side to side
as a tree moving in the wind,
like a mother's heartbeat
felt by the child in her womb
back and forth
back and forth

I fought sleep
that threatened to overtake me
hungry and scared
once more so terrible alone
squished between the wooden sidewall
and a fat, big woman
with a basket in her lap.
The wagon was overcrowded
I tried to make myself invisible
the voices around me thundered against my mind
they were all German
My hands cramped around the handle of my little red suitcase
my feet hurt
the boots were too small
shaped after another child's feet
not mine
behind my eyes
the heap of abandoned shoes on the Umschlagsplatz
stormed my mind

. . . .
I swallowed and swallowed
a big lump in my throat,
telling myself
don't cry
DON'T CRY

My nostrils caught a strange
but familiar smell
Food!
No doubt—
it was food!
Here,
food?
The woman next to me busied herself with the content of the basket
Suddenly it seemed that everybody around me
were chewing, smacking
the noise of their eating
hit my stomach
the hungry wolf inside was not asleep anymore . . .
my mouth watered
I swallowed
and swallowed
couldn't recall the last time
the wolf was fed
I stared wide-eyed at all the delicacies disappearing in the big gap
I chewed
and chewed
and swallowed

Then she came back aware of my look
angry she screamed at me
her eyes like black coal
My fingers tightened around the name tag
hanging around my neck
brought it slowly to my hungry mouth,
its dry taste reminded me of Jiri
and the crusts of black bread
shared in the safety of the darkness
under our blanket
deep into the night.
As the train continued its journey through the unknown night
the worst horror of them all
came to me
the witness of my sucking
had erased the address
and my name
inked on the tag

Cold,
a-lone
trembling
and hungry
I huddled in the corner
To the accompany of the wheels
a-lone
a-lone

What are we going to do with this trash?
I recognized the SS man by his voice
I dared not to look up
I lay there among all the dead bodies
Look, there is one moving, he yelled
he is moving, the stinking corpse
Cold sweat broke out all over me
I wanted to cry out:
No, not this way—
please . . .
I want to be with mama . . . .
a single shot rang out
followed by a dull groan
then all quiet again . . . .
I inched along the ditch
knocking into and crawled over cold and stiff bodies
and now. I knew
they were dead . . .
My hands were smeared with their blood
I kept away from the Sonderkommando
who were launching the dead into the ovens.
When they were nearby I froze
as if I were dead
waited
until they passed

The crematorium fire flared up
higher and higher
I crawled on . . . .
on . . . .
on . . . .
somebody grabbed me from behind:
panic went through me—
then a voice
angry
the lovliest voice
JIRI

Jiri, Jiri I whispered as I recognized him
He took a long step towards me
For a moment his eyes seemed to light up,
then
it passed,
his eyes peered into mine,
clouded with hopelessness
I am hungry
I want to eat . . . .
give me something . . . .
please Jiri,
I know you can . . .
horrified he looked at me
then slowly closed his eyes
he sobbed once . . . .
it was still night

I don't know when I first knew:
maybe it was when I understood that the loud voices outside
the block were not my father and mother quarreling in the dark—
but the hoarse voices of the SS and Kapos—
another trainload had arrived, and the air would be fat and sticky again.

I woke up in the night, again and again,
hot, like I was going to have a fever
and I wanted to call my mother,
to feel her holding me tight, to smell her body and knowing I was safe.
But I couldn't even get out a wimp,
she would not be there
everything was impossible and scaring
—and strange . . . .
So I had to make myself wholly awake
even I didn't want to
sit straight in the bed
and become like an empty shell
my head would swell and swell, keeping the empty shell afloat
in the room
my ears like doors in an abandoned house, their locks damaged, the
wind slamming them back and forth-back and forth.

I have been to the pit . . .
there was nothing
except the smell and stiff dead bodies
Jiri pushed me to the edge forcing me to look down
he laughed,
laughing into my ears:
do you see? Do you see her-our mama?
Standing there, it began to thunder behind my eyes
I couldn't move
far away Jiri's voice was thin and filled with panic, calling me back
calling my name.

Hands,
hands coming in the dark
big hard hands
foundling, hurting
afterwards I just managed to reach the Scheiserei
before it was too late
sometimes it was . . . .

But the Scheiserei was safe
and big
I could sit there for a long time
in the dark
just sitting there
until the cold made my body stiff
or
somebody was coming

I felt I needed to go,
Pulling at Jiri's sleeve
to tell him,
but he stood there, talking
and talking
he was big then
and didn't see me
then it started to go through my clothes
first it felt warm
and not bad at all
but it was wrong
one of the boys saw what was happening
and told Jiri
they all laughed
pointing fingers
laughed
their open mouths got bigger and bigger
their laughing voices louder and louder
until it filled my head and body
and the whole world
I dragged into my shame
quite alone
against everybody

But that was not the worst

My stomach exploded
it just came
and I couldn't hold it back
I felt the pressure
how it trickled down my legs
down to the floor

The boys laughed even harder,
sniffed and made faces at Jiri who couldn't manage his stupid little
sister
I trembled somewhere inside me,
but I hold my body stiff,
it slowly trickled down
my legs
to the floor
thin, thin, yellow filth . . .

I can still feel how something broke
Something which would never stop breaking
I can still feel the smell
of myself
and see the brown stained legs
remembering the wide open gasps around me
pouring out laughter
filling me with shame

At the Revier, the Putzerin let me know that it was God who had
made up the shame.
I was not really sure what she meant, was it: Herr Doktor?
or somebody in the sticky smoke the SS shouted at and always
lifted their fists up to: Herr Heil Hitler?
That made it hopeless,
because it was something one wouldn't escape
not even to think about.
God had made that somebody should be ashamed
because it was for your own good . . . .
sinful dirty creature as you were
and I understood I was one of them . . .
I lied when it was convenient,
Snatched other's food when nobody was around.

But I wondered how it could be that there were people around looking
as if there was nothing to be ashamed of in the whole world
and I knew what they did
all of us knew
would always know.

I never knew
that children play
with dolls and stuffed pets and the like,
I thought that childrens play
is bones of the dead,
and the best of them
are the ones from you mother,
or maybe from your little sister.
You polish them with the hem of your Lager clothing,
carefully you spit on it,
and you move your fingers
in small circles
and the bone will be like
the silk of her hair
smooth to your skin
when you play with it,
your mother plays with you
she will always be there—
for you
the secret joy of knowing
the Kapos and the SS
will never see
that your whole family is here
watching all what they do
even Herr Doktor
all knowing and all powerful as he is
cannot see my father standing here
But sometimes,
by dark—
or when I have nothing in my stomach,
the smooth, silky bone between my fingers
hidden well,
out of sight,
makes me cry.

For a brief moment I felt again
the hard grip of Herr Doktor's hands
then I couldn't see
for the burning red behind my eyes
fire was everywhere
I turned to the door, wanted to run
but to run
I had to breathe
Without realizing
I inhaled the burning sear
Sucking the flames deep
igniting my lungs
there was pain
like nothing I had ever experienced
there was no air
to breathe either in or out
not even to scream
all I knew was
that I was in fire
and that I was running
then time itself began to slow
I could see the door
the sky outside the window
and Antigone in her pink chair
strangely and despite the terrible pain
now seeming to exist in every part
of me
I felt a deep peace
Never mind what had ever happened in my life
I knew
that for me
the disease that had
ultimately
usurped my soul
was going
to be
terminated

that the cost was enormous
didn't count
in a matter of moments
I would be free
and
alive

Today I killed Dr. Mengele
He shall not torment my body anymore
he shall not hunt me, or experiment on me
He is dead
he is dead
I can leave the Kinderblock
If I can find the way—
He is dead
the worms eat him now
he is dead
it is like a song
he is dead
I am still afraid
but it all happeneda long time ago
and I am safe now
he cannot do anything
he is dead
I think I will kill him again
and again—
kill him for my brother
kill him for my mother
kill him for my Tate
kill him for all the tears
I could never cry
kill him for my little Rebecca
make him most dead
I shall dance slowly and grave
for all my dead friends.

Die Putzerin

We had many nicknames, we who lived in the Kinderblock
Jiri, my beloved brother,
was named the Putzerin.
I liked it—
it had such a sweet taste,
and it was also true;
Jiri always cared about me and the way I looked.
He would spit on the hem of his jacket and clean my face
when I came from Dr. Mengele.
"Sauberkeit uber alles."
He looked after me, and was really like the Putzerin. The Putzerin
was a nurse's aide who tried somehow to keep the Revier clean.
But Jiri hated the name, and I couldn't understand why.
—One evening, it was quite late; I could not sleep. Jiri was not there
and I trembled with fear because he was not in bed with me.
Somehow-I must have slept;
But then,
A sudden sound.
I sat up, tense.
What was it?
A hissing noise,
terrible and scaring
thundered in my ears.
It was a whispering voice, wheezing terrible, forbidden words:
YID, YID
Putzerin
The Putzerin is aroysgevorfen (thrown out)
Momzer (bastard)
Pisher (bedwetter)
YID, YID
I held my hands tight, so the words should not pierce me,
and
there was Jiri . . .
a silent, dark shadow slipping beneath the blanket—
silent and cold.
Jiri . . . I called—
JIRI . . .

he laid there, tense and stiff.
Jiri, Jiri—
my hand searching his face—
it was wet,
he was crying . . .
I panicked . . .
Jiri cried . . .
Suddenly I understood:
why Jiri hated the word-he was the pleasure for the old man
in the Sonderkommando—
like I had to be,
sometimes.
Damn the alter kocker . . . fuck him . . . .
damn him . . .
the bed was cold that night—
but Jiri sang me to sleep:
sh-sh Bubeleh
sh-sh
but even in my sleep, I heard:
YID, YID . . .

They hanged him there,
my brother Jiri
they hanged him
between the heavens and the earth
they hanged him
one
long
long
scream
it sounded like it lasted a thousand years—
maybe it did
my brother Jiri
they hanged him
he screamed
he should have been silent
like a lamb on its way to the slaughter
but he screamed

and I looked on
my eyes dry
he screamed
as I did
when the train pulled out
he hanged there
between the heavens and the earth
his body penduling
like a grandfather's clock—
tic-toc, tic-toc . . .

they hanged him, my brother Jiri
they hanged him.

I could not see Jiri,
but now they brought him out
from somewhere
in a bunch of soldiers.
They shuffled him into the empty space
in front of the gallows.
There were two others, they were old,
and had sacks over their heads—
I wondered what it was like to be inside of that—
was it hot and did it itch?
I wanted desperately to call Jiri again,
but my mouth was dry,
and I could not get the words out.

And then,
They hanged him . . .

The SS botched the job—
he sprung the trap, but the fall was not long enough—
Jiri's neck did not break—
He was not heavy enough.
I saw him swinging
under the gallow,
choking to death.
A Kapo crawled underneath
and pulled on his legs.

By then I had stopped screaming,
and only stood there and looked.
Jiri's eyes were open,
and he made this terrible noise
as if he had a piece of bread in his windpipe.

When they took him down
he was still alive—
he lay there
shaking and thrashing about,
his knees jerking up and down.

He lay on his belly on the muddy ground—
when they flopped him over on his back
and stabbed him
his bowels fell out
and hung there in a bloody mess—
the smell was terrible,
he had shit his pants
and the stain spread down his legs . . .
That was what I remember the most;
I could not stand that smell . . . .
As they dragged me away,
Jiri went on jerking
as the blood pumped out in a steady, dark stream—
when they shut the train door behind me
he had stopped jerking . . . .

I had to hide
Jiri found a nice, dark hole opposite where the wagons were that they used for
feeding the ovens.
It was close to the brick stone wall of the crematorium oven, also.
I was warm
I think I slept most of the time.
Hungry too
more than I had ever been
but Jiri was there
that counted more than anything else.
After a while, the Schafer inside me stopped barking.
It became more like the snoring in the Kinderblock by night time.
I asked Jiri for something to eat
But he sneared: You want food also?
What in Hell you think I am?
The Messiach?
I dared not to answer
that was just what I was thinking he was.
It helped to put a stone in my mouth.
I made pictures inside my head
what food it could be . . . .
I don't know how long I had been there.
I think I had slept
looking out,
I saw the SS who used to tell me about his little daughter, and give
me candy.
He used to give me other things too,
not so nice things.
I was happy to see him
and was just about to crawl out
when I saw him talking to Jiri.
Jiri looked so strange, that I halted
and waited to see what was happening.
When I saw Jiri pulling down his pants
my heart almost stopped beating.
At first I could see the SS only from the back,
and I wondered what he was doing.
Suddenly he stepped
over Jiri-was almost sitting on him.
That big SS and Jiri—
what game were they playing?
They looked exactly like the dogs when they mated.

My eyes get big,
I wanted to look,
but somehow I knew I saw something I should not see.
It was scaring;
the noises they made
especially the SS.
Jiri sounded like one of the small dogs when the Kapos kicked them.
I backed into my hole, and waited for Jiri.
My mouth dry and my chest hurting.
There he was, Jiri . . .
Eagerly I asked him:
are you going to be his dog? (that was the best which could happen, dogs
always had food).
I pointed at Lars, the SS.
He was on his way over the the blocks.
When I closed my mouth;
Jiri got a look in his eyes, making me so afraid that I made a yellow
puddle between my feet.
He got wild.
He hit me with his fists, so I could hardly keep standing.
I really don't want to tell how long and how hard he was beating me.
First my mouth and my nose were bleeding,
and my jacket became wet with blood.
He suddenly stopped.
He collapsed into a little pile
and he cried without a sound of tears.
His mouth and face twisted so I could hardly recognize it.
I sat beside him without a word.
Holding his sleeve, I knew nothing would ever, never comfort him.

One day, two days after, they hanged him.

"From The Uncaptive Mind . . . ."

One of the boys we feared most, was Jankele.
He was Polish, tall with small cold eyes.
We feared him because he was "in" with the Blockalteste, and when
somebody was beaten up, he so clearly enjoyed it.
He was a gossiper too, O ja, we feared him.
And he hated Jiri, jealous because both Jiri and I could read so well.
One day the whole matter exploded:
he found Jiri reading;
Jankele snickered, twisting the tip of his little finger back and forth
in his nostril-rubbed his finger on the sleeve of his jacket and
laughed.
"What a waste . . . You do not need book learning in this finery."
"You do if you want to become stronger than the SS."
"Oh, you think you will . . . someday? You REALLY do . . ."
Jiri's lips lost color:
"I shall be damned if I become so poor and stupid as you . . ."
Jankele bellowed and started toward Jiri.
I let off my nervous stirring on my soup bowl hanging in its string tied
around my waist.
Hands extended, I rushed to Jankele:
"He did not mean that. Be good as the rabbi taught us we should . . . ."
"Stupid little bitch . . . I will deal with him as I want," shouted Jankele.
And he cuffed me on the side of my head.
I staggered, slammed my shoulder hard against the iron stove in the midst
of the room, cried out.
The pain somehow destroyed my allegiance to the rabbi.
My eyes flew wide open as Chaim, the skinny cross eyed boy next to our bunk,
spied the fallen poker, snatched it and raised it to threaten Jankele.
It was a pathetic gesture, but Jankele chose to see it as one of great menace;
he turned on him.
Frightened and angry Jiri wrestled with the much bigger Jankele, trying to
protect skinny Chaim. But Jankele beat him off.
Chaim terrified, tumbled with the poker, unable to get a firm grip on it.
So Jankele easily ripped it from his hand and while Jiri and I silently
watched, used it to hit Chaim twice on his temple.
And Chaim sprawled on his face with streaks of blood running down his check.
Except for us the room was empty.
Jiri stared at him for a moment.

then in uncontrolled rage, lunged for the poker.
Jankele laughing threw it against the wall.
Jiri ran to the stove, seized the kettle chain-the Kapos and Blockalteste
used to make coffee there-flung the hot kettle over Jankele, who screamed
and pressed his hands to his scalded eyes.
Jiri's hands were burned also, but it looked like he hardly noticed it.
He raised the empty kettle and smashed it against Jankele's head.
when he fell, Jiri wrapped the chain around his neck and pulled it until
it ws half embedded in the flesh.
Jankele finally stopped kicking and lay still.
Grabbing my hand, we ran out in the mist and vomited.
I could feel Jiri's hands were burning.
Staring at each other, we both realized what he had done
and we wanted to cry and run away.
But we did not.
We forced ourselves toward the open door.
Once inside the barrack again, we saw Chaim's back moving slowly.
he was alive . . . .
After many attempts, Jiri got him on his feet.
He muttered-incoherently and laughed.
Jiri put his arm around his shoulder and guided him out the door and
down the misty lane to the only shelter we knew: the Shiesseri.
I followed slowly, afraid to be left behind.
On our way, Chaim faltered several times, but Jiri's urgent plea, kept
kept him going.
The children there gathered around us, and Meir, one of the biggest, examined
Chaim;
then stood back, fingering his lips.
"We need somebody," Jiri cried.
But none could conceal his worry.
"He is badly hurt" . . . .
Jiri was stunned, bringing his tears at last:
"That cannot be" . . . .
"Look at him . . . he is hardly breathing . . . we can do nothing for him and we
will only be questioned about the cause of his injuries."
The statement itself was a kind of question.
Jirr had only blurted out that Jankele had hit him.
"All what we can do is to wait," concluded Meir, rubbing an eye.
"And pray;" Jiri said out of his desperation.
I prayed with every bit of my being.
There was no sign the prayer was heard . . . .

Chaim's breathing grew slower, feebler, although he survived until we could
hear the evening apell over the roofs.
Jiri and I slowly went back to the Kinderblock.
Jiri held my hand so tight that it hurt and the skin turned white.
My heart pounded in my throat:
Had anybody seen?
Was the Angel of Death there?
Der schwartze Mann?
Nobody had seen.
It was a great fuss around the block.
And they carried away Jankele's body.

Meir never spoke to us again . . . . Never . . . .

The view was from the operating table straight up to the bright floodlights that gave off a glow of heat that warmed my forehead uncomfortably. Each face that loomed over me was masked with a white mask which covered nose and mouth, above which strained concentrating eyes. The cold eyes in charge were Dr. Mengele's, I could recognize along with the hard voice that crackled commands to his team mates.
I closed my eyes slowly and held myself quiet.
He turned my head, pressing my cheek hard against the white sheet, and his strong hands were reminiscent of my long forgotten father turning my head, to check the cleanness of my ears after my evening sponge bath.
I felt the panic sweep through my body and I was suddenly violently arching my back in terror-charged strain against the restraining straps.
For God's sake, hold her; yelled Herr Doktor, and all hands pressed me to the table. Only my head was free. I screamed, but no sound was coming out of my mouth. What had they done to me? I strained against the straps. Each arm was pinned down-a strap across my legs just above my knees and another one across my chest.
Through the panic I felt embarrassed because my bowels let go, but that was instantly drowned in an overwhelming terror.
No . . . no . . . I screamed and still no sound came from me, No . . . no . . . my body arched the opposite way now. My head twisted to the left. My cheek pressed against the table in the incredible effort to turn my head face down to protect myself from the awful glowing blade too close—
then I blacked out
I sat upright.
free
their faces gone.
The room was dark.

I am afraid.
The other children too.
Herr Doktor and the SS are smiling, all the time.
It is not really smiling—
Herr Doktor looks like a big, dangerous Schafer; I can see his teeth.
I would feel better if they all were angry-as they used to.
I try to hide behind the other-to be invisible.
The SS say something about food:
Shall we have something to eat???
My stomach is growling—
there has been nothing to eat since the last transport arrived.
There has been a lot of noise—
the smoke from the crematories is black and sticky.
There must be many Luftmenschen by now.
Jiri is also busy.
He is in the Sonderkommando
And he is useful—
always be useful-that is the rule of the block—
he is useful: his hands have just the right size for pulling out
difficult teeth from the dead.
The SS like gold—
I do not understand why. You cannot eat gold, can you?
Herr Doktor is away a lot,—
We know new transports are coming; he is at the
train station all the time.
So they are leaving us alone. But you have to behave. Don't get attention

Just behave . . .

But there is no soup,
or bread,
or anything else to eat, when new transports are coming.
There is like a hard, ugly knot inside me.
I am so hungry that I have tried to eat mud, from where
people vomit outside the Shieserei. But it only made me more sick.
So now—
they talk about food . . .
it makes me scared;
I do not like the way Herr Doktor and the others look like,
best to keep an eye on them . . .

It was quiet in the Kinderblock,
so quiet it could be
just before you
had to get up.
All that you heard.
was moaning and small whimps,
and words you could hardly figure out what they meant.
Words never spoken
when awake:
mama-mama—
come-mama . . .
it is so dark—
mama . . .
I am afraid . . .
. . . mama . . .

I was awake
and tense
Jiri snored,
and turned in bed—
—I sat up:
the door chrinched,
a dark shadow slipped in,
without a sound;
who could it be?
Der Schwartze Mann?
He was usually tight to the window behind Herr Dorktor, (the windows were
painted over with black) but we feared der Schwartze Mann
more than anybody else,
If he came in his big, black mantle.

Obedient, I followed her. The Lager was silent
it was cold and very dark.
—I was afraid
not because I knew we were going to see Herr JDoktor,
I knew very well what that meant,
but the strange hour
and even more,
the unexpected kindness:
she let me hold her hand,

tight—
I think, her holding my hand
scared me
more than anything else could.

I thought I was a big girl—
big—
sometimes I felt even bigger than Jiri.
I was proud when he said I was a big girl.
Other times,
when I was in Herr Doktor's strong-smelling office,
I could tell myself
all the time—
almost all lthe time—
I am a big girl.
Even when I get Schieserei and spoiled my clothes
or vomited
or cried
I could still
inside me
believe I was a big girl.
This night it did not work.
I felt very little
and scared.

As we walked
the echo of her wooden clogs
went back and forth
between the walls of the blocks.
We walked forever.

Outside the door
she halted—
kissed me lightly on my forehead,
before she opened the door,
and suddenly became
one of the angry grown-ups again.
My eyes blinked against the sudden light,
that hurt my eyes.

They grabbed me,
Lifted me up on the table
under the big lamp
and strapped me down
I said nothing,
clinched my teeth
and held my breath.
The straps were so tight
That they went deep-into my skin
it hurt . . . .
Even then I said nothing,
I coud not breathe—
the world stood still.

I looked at the bright lamp
above me—
at the shinny metal things on the little table next to me—
Herr Doktor put something red on his hands;
very careful—
I think he loved his hands the most of everything in the Lager—
He stood there
and looked at me,
I could see his dark eyes above his mask
glowing like the night outside.

The sharp pain
came so suddenly
that it took me completely by surprise—
the cut was deep and long.
I closed my eyes.
Somebody put in a piece of cloth
between my teeth.
It was dry and sticky
I wanted to spit it out,
but they would not let me.
I groaned and twisted,
trying to get away from the terrible pain
going deeper and deeper inside me.
It was red and white,
and blue.

I cried.
I was ashamed
not being a big girl.
All what I wanted
was my mami
. . . she was not there . . .
I was alone in this pain . . .
I do not know what I did—
—or what they did—
all that I know;
it hurt
more than anything else.

They pulled up my legs—
did something between them,
beyond pain—
beyond everything—
it burned and hurt—
It was like
I could look at myself,
being somewhere else,
dirty and bloody . . .
I vomited
and vomited
gagged
and vomited
they had to take out
the cloth in my mouth.
They loosened the straps,
sitting there,
I dared not to move . . . .
Herr Doktor looked at me with his night dark eyes:
I was not his big girl,
and I would get no candy.

I cried for Jiri,
Whimpered for my mami,
I was alone . . .
The big people around me had no mouths,
nor ears,
only cold eyes.

The memory of the kiss had faded away,
and was gone . . .

Herr Doktor was there
he said nothing
his hands moved . . .
my body became numb
I could feel
nothing—
no more.

It was a terrible stank.
I knew the smell came from me.
I screamed for Jiri
for mami . . .
Exhausted,
I whispered Jiri's magic formula:
Shema Israel, Adonai Eloheinu . . . .
Herr Doktor ripped off his mask
slapped me over my mouth,
once—
twice—
and left angry.
My Schieserei went on and on . . .
I sat there . . .
waiting.

Waited and waited . . .
Watching the other children,
heard them cry.
I just sat there.
Nobody paid attention to me the whole, endless day.

Then one of the SS ordered me
to stand up:
Herr Doktor wanted to speak to me,
I tried to stand straight,
you should not lift your head
but I did . . . .
The window was dark,

I close to
cried,
when he turned towards me:
Du hast mich verraten.
The words thundered in my ears—
—Du has mich virchlich verraten—
I trembled and said nothing—
HE was God.
He said:
—Du bist eine Judin
I knew my end was close.
I screamed,
A long, soundless
ugly scream
He WAS God.
—Ich wollte dir eienes neues Identitat geben—
I heard the words,
And understood nothing.
But I felt it in my inner bones
what it meant.
—Aber Ich habe blaue Augen,
Ich kann nicht eine dreckiger Jude sein—
I knew it was hopeless.
I had betrayed him.
When I whimped the Shema,
I betrayed him—
When I clinched my teeth together not to scream—
I betrayed him.
Because I did not say a word
when the pain was red and white
and pounded behind my eyes.
I betrayed HIM.
when I called for my mami,
and not for him
I betrayed him.
when the SS wanted me to dance,
I betrayed him.
It was for HIM I should have danced—
so I betrayed him.
When I could not carry my dark secrets any longer,

the burden of my love to him
I betrayed him
as I did when I failed his last, big experiment
I betrayed him.
His kingdom was of this world,
his message immortal.
Not three times
but every time I refused
to scream for HIM
to hail HIM king
When I let be known to him my love
I was to know
I meant nothing to him
not even as a number—
I betrayed him.
When I paint him
and every touch of my brushes on my canvas
is as his hands;
causing me more pain
than all the experiments
and I still go on
painting—
I betray him—
Yet I paint—
senseless—
as in a trance—
If I stop
I will betray
my dead comrades,
who did scream.

With these screams in my ears,
I turned towards the desk;
the big, brown desk
covered with papers,
the lists of our numbers—
mine among them—
I could not help it,
but face him—
as I stood there, looking up in Herr Doktor's eyes—
I knew it was hopeless.
His eyes were dark,
he did not move.
I waited.
Suddenly he shouted, screamed so loud that I jumped:
Enough . . .
Get out of here . . .
Schnell . . .
The SS who had taken a firm grip on my neck tightened his grip.
He grumbled something . . .
I was not sure if it was "dreckiger Jude"
or
"drerckiger Doktor"
But of course,
THAT could not be.
And I was afraid.
Even I knew about the Luftmenschen,
and death, and the crematories, and the gas chambers;
how you became a Luftmensch,
I did not know
exactly . . .
Every time I tried to ask, the other children hushed me down. And Jiri
looked so strange, I dared not ask again.
But now I would know, soon enough.
And I was afraid.
So afraid, that without thinking, I stopped in the middle of the Lager—
Strasse, and refused to take one step more.
The SS tried to make me move, he almost dragged my arm off—
but could not make me move.
Finally he lifted me up, and carried me like another package.
I dared not to kick or something like that,

but made my body stiff as I could.
I was angry also;
to be carried like I was a little child . . .
"I am big: BIG. Do you hear?
I am big.
Let me down
I can walk by myself.
I am big.
BIG."
But the SS was deaf, I think.
And there we were:
in the front of the big grey coloss,
known by all of us in the Kinderblock:
the gas chamber.
The SS let me down, and pushed me over to the group of people already
gathered there. I do not know how many:
children in all sizes,
grown-ups;
many.
There were the SS and the Kapos. All shouting and screaming, pushing
and kicking.
I knew, I was very small and helpless.
Small . . .
A Kapo screamed that I should take off my clothes.
Take away my clothers?
Not for my life.
Even when the Kapo gave me a slap so hard that I saw lights and white
and red, I hanged on to my clothes. I needed them, I was going to America—
Didn't he know that?
He gave up . . .
I looked at the other children: it must be their mama, I thought.
And felt a pang of jealousy as I watched the children in their mother's
arms.
Becoming a Luftmensch would be easy if you were with you mama.
There was so much noise and smell, and . . . .
Nobody paid attention to me, not even the Kapos.
I felt terribly alone,
Jiri was gone,
I was alone,
for the first time in my life, I was alone.

And I was to become a Luftmensch.
Because I had failed Herr Doktor . . .
I am alone . . .
Alone.
It is cold. I shiver.
Try to move closer to an old woman with a little one in her lap.
I move closer to her.
Only little by little,
so she will not notice and kick me away.
Careful, careful . . .
But her eyes are empty.
She looks through me.
Maybe that is what it is?
To be a Luftmensch.
That people look through you,
not seeing you . . .
The screaming and yelling suddenly raise to a storm.
Look:
the big doors are open.
Mama, help me . . .
Jiri . . . Jiri
JIRI
I shall be so good
Please.
. . . Jiri . . . NO
We are inside.
How can all of us have room?
I curl myself to a ball—
hold my hands over my head.
I do not want to see anything—
or hear anything—
I do not want to feel anything—
But nothing helps.
I cannot close out anything . . .
The smell—
the cries—
the screams—
the door is closed—
people push and kick—
slap me—

somebody is standing on my back:
it hurts—
Ima-it hurts
please . . .
it hurts . . .
Something is thrown in,
Look:
there is an opening up there . . .
Somebody screams:
GAS . . .
Do not open your mouth . . .
DON'T BREATHE . . .
FOR HEAVENS SAKE . . .
DON'T BREATHE . . .
But I have to . . .
and I let in a little in a gasp.
A terrible pain in my throat. Never, ever I have felt such pain . . .
Never . . .
It is like a sharp whiteness goes through my chest—
my stomach twists.
The smell—
I must throw up—
Jiri . . .
Mami . . .
Jiri, I cannot help I am soiling myself . . .
Jiri, I shall never do it again . . . I promise.
Jiri:
it is so dark here . . .
Jiri . . .
It hurts—
IT HURTS
. . . help me . . .
HELP ME-please . . .
TATA?
Am I in Shul?
There comes the song from?
Shema Israel-Adonai Eloheinu . . . Adonai . . . .
Jiri—
stop it please?
The red and the white.

See the blue . . .
and the green . . .
the pain in my throat . . .
I cannot stop it . . .
My head . . .
do not smash my head . . . ,
who is it?
Help me . . .
PLEASE . . .
I have to breathe . . .
I have to . . .
DO YOU HEAR?
I HAVE TO . . .
Jiri . . . .
let me breathe . . .
please . . . plea . . . . pl . . . .

Had I left my only home to follow
A blind illusion,
a desperate dream?
I am on my way to some distant harbor,
but despite the glittering lights from the city behind
and the noise and dazzling sounds of the living
I feel as alone.
As the small lighthouse against the horizon
drifting toward the darkness beyond.
Why was I left behind?
Why are you calling on me
this way
now?
Are you really out there?
wailing?
Are you so alone
as I am?
Are you lost,
did you have to die that day?
Did you look back with tears in your eyes
and having second thoughts
didn't you remember how much I loved you?
How much I needed you?
Could you just erase the sight of me
running into your arms,
gazing up at you with so much love
and so much need?

And when you turned and looked
toward the future
was it really a future without me
forever without me?

I am coming for my answers

I have come to the end of daylight,
faced the doorway of darkness.
When I touched my face
my eyes were closed
and my chin cold.

All that I thought I loved and needed
was just gone.
I was naked
and
shivered in misery.

They were measuring me for the coffin.
Suddenly
I heard a voice
calling from within.
I turned my eyes
to look back
to look down
to look deep.
There was a single candle
it drew me close
until I could reach out
and put my fingers in the flame
Slowly
slowly, I burned away.
My dead
when they were gone
I was no longer naked.

How can one measure the distances one has travelled?
What use are the personalities of one's old Self—
To comprehend them?

Soon,
I firmly resolve.
I will gather up my courage
and join the present human time,
leaving the old garments behind.

And
despite all this,
I will still mourn,
And weep for this lost part of myself.
Always feel sad for a land
I cannot return to.
A land doubly inaccessible now.

But the weeping is buried deeply,
perhaps lodged in the one area
It is illegal to modify

How ironic then
that in this way the prisoned child from the thousand light years of yesterday
will remain
As long as any part of me exists
there this little girl will be with me.
Because I share the destiny
and the past
with this noble, mysterious, small people
from the House of Death,
I feel continuity,
and an urge for the stars;
indeed more than that:
a drive for the present.

Somewhere the dim portions of my memory
informs me
how I as a child asked how long people would live
if they got to heaven.

And they said
perhaps so long as they wish.
Perhaps a billion years.
How long is a billion years I asked?
It is a very long time they said.

An age,
an eternity
but time enough for all life to rise
and all life to end.

In geological terms
I learned later:
a billion years is indeed an ae'on
But the Greeks who coined the word
were not so specific.
They used it as a pointer to eternity,
the lifetime of a universe is far more than a billion years.
It was also the personification of a god's cycle of time.

I have survived the House of Silence,
as I have survived the end of my universe,
I might survive others.

So much still to learn
so much change to look forward to.

Each day I can breathe more deeply.

I count my choices and realize
I will be free

And alone.

Tata, Mein Tata

Lord spoke and said
your wife
your son
your little daughter
only one
loved of you
go to the land
I will show you
another one.
I bring you where you don't want
to go
another one will handle your body
another
one you don't know.
I take your mantle
uncover your shame.
There is nothing you can do
your wife
your son
your little daughter
only one
loved
little girl with pearling laughter
I witness your shame
carry it
her coat
the years to come
carry your shame on her shoulders
there was no angel
do not harm her
the knife fell from the hand
of your wife
your son
your only son
beloved
hung in the tree
the ram provided

for the burnt offering
your little daughter
your pride and hope

is still among the living.

Just ears and yes
My body was tense and alert

In all its monstrous self-confidence
And knowledge of its power
The fear became one with me
I waited
I waited
Patience I had more than enough
Sharp sight and hearing I seldom lacked

I waited
My patience would last long enough
But the sweet rage
Always stayed shortly with me

When thoughts started to grind
I tried to hold on to the white rage
But had to give in
Let it go away

Then
The thoughts came back
They consumed the rage
Just as I knew they would

But the rage had given me strength
I felt as I started to walk again

My heart leaped for joy
When I suddenly heard a river
I ran the last few meters
And stood thee
In the middle of the waterfall

Slowly letting myself cool off
Became clean
And dripping wet
Quenched my thirst
Let down my hair
Undressed
The damp clothes went
One by one
Washed them through
Hung them on the rock to dry

Standing naked in the middle of the sunshine
I looked at the world

At that moment everything forgotten
Only acknowledging the yearning
Through the years
For just such a moment

The memories called me
The childhood country was there
Within reach

How could it be
That I remembered?
Why all these pictures
Of parents
My brother
Friends
Events
Places
Meetings
Disappointments
Pain and joy?

Was it because nobody had allowed me to name them?
It was so easy for others to deny me a past
My memories couldn't exist if there were no words
What existed then
Outside the words

Something was there
Not outside the words
But behind them
Beyond them

And I was on my way to find out

You
He said
His voice carrying what his eyes told
For so long I can remember
You, he said
And touched my throat
My face

He has such beautiful eyes
Dark with glittering and playfulness
Deep within
Curious, searching
And a little afraid

He had such beautiful eyes
I corrected myself

Came the forbidden
The danger of aloneness
I forced myself to focus on the present
At the now
The merciful dark came
Embraced me
Whipped out all the forbidden thoughts
Made me finally able to close my eyes

He had died
They killed him
But the other part of him was left behind
Him with the burning eyes I tried so hard to understand
He who was my brother too
And a stranger

Within was a pain
Ever stronger
Than the grief over my dead

They need to know

But not now
Always
Later
Believing and hoping
That sometimes
It was with pain as with thunder
It did not kill
Only frightened you

He would never come back

The one who lives only in the now
He has no memories
Does not have to struggle with the shadows of the past
The one who lives only now
Has no future
Has never to be afraid
Never to carry the burden of all these pictures
From the House of Death
But for me there would always be the long time ago
The pictures others tell me
I better forget

There will always be a yesterday
And a tomorrow

A child had died
Its quiet darkness
Softly resting over its sad face

Dark and soft
But still afraid
And sad
Very sad

You will come back
He begged
They kill
You know that
But you will come back
Please

The feelings remembered
I did not expect to be welcomed
Outside the House of Death and Silence
Who would welcome me
When I could remember only a face
A name
The color of a voice
But no words for telling

I turned and lifted my hand
Quietly
With the palm towards him
Trust me
It meant
He stood there
Looking tired and alone
And scared
Very scared

Later, much later
As I rested in the sunshine
I knew
I had to make a decision
To remember
Or plunge ahead
But then
Pushed away the very thought
Later
I told myself

For a while I drifted away
But his eyes penetrated my rest
His frightened hands
The rope around his neck

And I screamed
A long soundless scream echoing
Inside

I was tired now
And hungry
My hand fumbled in my pocket
For a piece of bread

I would not sleep
I told myself
But in no-man's land
And being half asleep
The pictures came
Not the ones I hoped for
The difficult and cruel ones
From home
My mother's dying body
The little boy's body jerking in the gallow

And my fears

Let them come then
The pain a reminder
Of being alive
The price for having
Survived